C000182789

Metamorphosis

April 2019

Beautifully made speculative fiction

Metaphorosis

April 2019

edited by
B. Morris Allen

Metaphorosis Books

Neskowin

ISSN: 2573-136X (online)
ISBN: 978-1-64076-137-7 (e-book)
ISBN: 978-1-64076-138-4 (paperback)

April 2019

A Yellow Landscape

Sarah McGill

I dream of vast landscapes. The distance bends like cotton on a washing line or a rabbit vanishing down a hole. In my dream, women come, carrying brutally tined forks. Their hands crook around their bodies and somehow they are monstrous and too big. I walk, and I think I'm looking for a better landscape. Or only another landscape. This place is too wide and I pool borderless across it.

A woman draws her fork around her and says, "When I was a girl and I walked on the beach, I found a little house crusted in salt. I sat inside and ate lamprey and mint leaves. At dusk it flooded and I laughed, splashing my feet in the water. I grew into the shape of that house, ancient and mindful."

"My nana's house was a tent," I say and I am very proud. "I want to have walls like she did, but I don't know how to grow into the shape of a tent. She walked barefoot on the mountain with her mule. She made acorn flour and shouted *haloo haloo* to the thrushes in the valley." I am barefoot too.

"Well, it is good to love your great-grandmother. But there are loose rocks on mountain paths and tents aren't houses. They're unstable."

A woman says, "She must have been sad with no doorway to frame her and no walls to hold her. I suppose she was unhappy because she had no house to grow up in and learn to be herself."

I scratch the dirt with my toes and think they're wrong, but I don't know how. I don't know if Nana was happy. And I hadn't known that a tent wasn't a house. I wonder then what walls I can grow up into if not those. I turn around and walk away from their monstrous forks.

I lived in a house that wasn't my house, and I lived in a room that wasn't my room. Out the window was a hill the color of clay, covered in scrub. The bed was my cousin Mosi's, even though I slept in it with her. It was obvious it was hers because my blankets were yellow like soil. These were blue, like a bottomless lake. Mosi decided she liked blue when she went to school and the teachers told her the ocean was best. I kept my bird bones in a drawer with her shells and together we built white houses with bone frames and shell rooves.

Downstairs, someone knocked. Out the window, I saw it was a teacher and I hid in the cupboard in Mosi's room. The teacher came sometimes and said I had to go to school, but she couldn't come for me if I stayed in the cupboard. That's what my aunt said. She said the woman would always go away. That sounded true. The cupboard was the smallest place in the house that I could fit. I knelt, folded up over my knees. Sometimes it was suffocating.

My aunt told the teacher I didn't live in the scrubland. She said I lived with my parents in the mountains, even though that wasn't true and they were dead.

When the teacher left, my aunt came and knocked on the cupboard. She opened the door and I spilled out. I sprawled, my legs and arms going as far as they could, all the way until they knocked against the walls.

When I went down to dinner, my cousin jostled me out of my seat next to my aunt and I went to sit out of her reach.

"Did you take the mule up to the hill today?" my aunt asked.

I nodded. "I want the hill to be as tall as the mountain Nana lived on."

My aunt served out the partridge's breast meat with pine nuts and pennyroyal. "If it were a mountain, at the top you would find the circle tent in the cloud, just like the hero Oupa did when he went looking for Buzzard. He lives there now and teaches everyone who comes to him."

"Nana met Oupa," I said, clasping my hands very seriously. "She laid down under a blanket and in her dream she was a kestrel and flew to the top of the mountain. Oupa smiled when he saw her."

My aunt pressed her lips together. "She told that story a lot."

"I want to do that. In my dream, I'll be a buzzard." I added pepper and rosemary to my meat.

Mosi laughed, leaning back in her chair to slap the rug hanging on the wall. Every time she slapped it, she grabbed a little thread and pulled, so that someday it would unravel and she wouldn't be embarrassed when her teacher came for dinner and frowned at the black goats leaping over the mountaintops.

"My teacher said that if you jump from the roof, you'll die," Mosi said. "She says it's a lie that Warbler jumped from a gable and learned to fly."

"Birds learn to fly by jumping from their nests," my aunt said, her eyes down. She ate with her fingers, the grease running down her palms. "You used to like the legends about Oupa."

"My teacher said bird meat is dirty." Mosi wrinkled her nose at the plate and wouldn't eat.

My aunt picked over her plate and I wished she'd say Mosi was wrong, but she said nothing.

In my dream, the sand is unfamiliar. Each time I kneel, I stand up far away from where I was a moment ago. I hate it.

I'm looking for Oupa. I think, far away, I see a mountain the color of sky. If I find it, I will find him and he'll teach me all the mountain's stories and how to be a buzzard. I don't look at the women when they come up behind me, although the terrible scraping of their forks makes my shoulders rise and my spine tingle.

"The wind is hard on my face," a woman says. "It burns my cheeks."

"You should wear a scarf like my aunt," I say. "It binds up her hair and keeps off the wind."

"Why don't you wear a scarf?" she says.

I put my hands up and I'm startled to find my hair uncovered, whipping around in the wind. "I lost it. I'll get another scarf, when I go home."

"What if you lose that too?"

For some reason I can't answer the question. It's too startling. Instead I ask, "If a tent isn't a house, then why does Oupa live in a tent?"

A woman laughs, so loud that the soil shakes from the mountain in the distance, cascading orange into the sand. The mountain is left bare and I see it's not a mountain, but only a rock, no taller than my hip. "Because he doesn't know anything at all," she says.

A woman spits. "It's too barren. Bring the ocean here."

I hunch my shoulder at the sprawling landscape. "I like the sand." But I reach into the soil where it's damp. A spring pops up as I pull back my hands.

A woman coos, "It makes me homesick. Oh, I miss squid."

Mosi came back to the house jumping, kicking up her legs to show off her new hard shoes. They glistened and I asked her if they were made of beetle carapaces.

"No," she said, and then wouldn't tell me what they were made of. She put her hands on her hips. "I'm going to the ocean."

"The mountain is better. In my dreams I'm going to the mountain."

"You don't really go places in your dreams."

I hurled sand over her shoes so they got dirty. "I do." I was so angry I almost hit her. "Just like Nana. I go somewhere else and you're not there."

"I'm going for real. My teacher says I'll like the ocean so much, I won't want to come back."

I crouched down in the sand. "Why did they come here, if they don't like it?" Many people came inland to escape the encroaching shoreline, the floods making the borders on the old maps all wrong, but there were still people near the ocean.

She licked her palms and leaned over to clean off her shoes. "Because they want to teach us to be good. The mountain people don't know how to be good. But if I go to school on the beach, I can be better."

"It'd be a long walk back in the evening."

She laughed and it was like the women with their forks laughing. "I wouldn't come home in the evening."

I held my hands in a cage at my belly, horrified. I didn't want to sleep in a house that was nearly empty, the wind rattling the loose windowpanes, or eat with just my aunt and the dripping dishes. "You aren't going."

She wrinkled her nose. "Yes I am."

"I said you can't go."

"I don't care." She clapped her hands in my face, like my aunt did when she was angry.

I pushed her hands away. "Your mama won't let you."

"It doesn't matter what she wants."

I lunged, grabbing her through her sweater. She hit me in the nose as we fell and she screamed about dirtying her uniform. I squeezed her around the waist. I imagined the empty house again and shook all over. I didn't want Mosi to leave me. I tried to map her body to mine, to match her concave belly over my hip, her spine around my arm. But she squirmed too much and when she hit my ear and set it ringing, I let go.

She scrambled to her feet, dust scrubbed into her uniform. Tears tracked down the dirt on her face. "I'm going to the ocean and I'm not coming back. No one can make me come back. I'll go to school there and be better than you." She turned and ran inside.

I curled up my knees and pretended I was in the cupboard, with the dark and the smell of pigeon. But it was too small, like I would never get out and would always be its cramped shape. I didn't want to grow into the shape of the cupboard. I sat up and wished a tent were a house.

My mule came around the house. She gnawed on the white shrubs beside me until I reached up and rubbed her flank. Her mane was full of dust. "Mosi doesn't mean it," I told the mule. "She won't leave. She'd miss the drawer with her little towels and the pegs to hang her shoes. The ocean is too wide and terrible for her." My mule gummed my hand.

When I came into the house, dirt up and down my knees, my aunt sighed. "I've told you not to jump on Mosi like that."

"She said bad things to me."

"What did she say?"

I didn't tell her. It would be more true if I said it. I would keep the words in my belly and make Mosi a liar. I sat in the corner and pretended it was a little house just for me.

"Can I sleep in the attic?" I asked while she stoppered the sink and poured in water. The attic had once been a dovecote. Doves were very sacred on the mountain, but I'd never seen one. "I'll sleep on a rug and hang walnuts and garlic like Nana did in the mountain."

My aunt shook her head. "I want Mosi to be in the room with you."

"Why? She doesn't get scared at night anymore. Not since her teacher told her

Owl doesn't come at night to steal children's tongues. She says owls are stupid and crabs are better, because their shells are their houses and they fit inside them perfectly."

My aunt muttered something I didn't understand, which sounded ugly and mean. "She's still very young."

"She doesn't like me sleeping with her. I want to sleep in the dovecote." The dovecote roof came to a point like a tent. But it wasn't a tent so it could be a good house where I could learn how to be myself.

She handed me a dish and I just held it. "I need it for storage," she said.

She started soaping the dishes and I held the plate tighter. "But there's nothing up there. Just old rugs and baskets."

She made a *tch* sound with her teeth that meant she was done arguing.

I set the plate into the water, holding it with the tips of my fingers, hoping it would float. It didn't. I scrubbed with the heel of my hand. I felt bad for being upset and hoped I could make my aunt smile. "Were there really doves?"

She put her hand on my shoulder. "A long time ago, when I was a girl. We ate dove when there were guests and to celebrate the day my father came down from the mountain. He said coming down was a good decision. The traders liked him, even though he didn't eat their fish."

I set the plates up to dry on the rack. "What happened to the doves?"

"When I was eleven, I told my teacher I didn't want to go to school anymore. She said I had to. Until I was sixteen, I would go to school. But I wanted to stay home and tend to the doves. My teacher came for dinner and she said we shouldn't eat bird. It made our bones brittle. It scared papa and he got rid of all the doves. Lots of other families were told to get rid of their doves too and soon all the doves were gone."

I rubbed my thumb on the tines of a fork and made faces at it. "Why would everyone give their doves away?"

She crooked her chin into her shoulder and whispered, "I found a dove with a bullet hole in its belly."

"What happened?"

"Not everyone agreed to get rid of their doves." Her shoulders lifted gently, with a kind of long-drawn weariness.

"Was Nana upset that you didn't have dove for her when she visited?"

She clattered a cup into the sink. "Very angry. She called papa a weak son. She said he didn't respect his family's traditions. That's why she took me out of school and brought me up to the mountain, even when the teachers sent men after her to bring me back. We stayed away from them for three years."

I smiled. I'd never lived in the mountains. My mother was a little girl when she came down with her family. I thought sometimes that nothing would be the same if I'd been born in a bed, with walls to hold me like a second womb. Or if I'd been born in a cave, held by stone and a sheet of rain across its mouth. But I was born in a gully and I tumbled out like water from a pipe. The shock of me spilled over and soaked the landscape. I was a flooded road, shallow and clear and so still it was like a hole into the sky.

My aunt's stories about the mountains made me proud and jealous. I wanted to climb a mountain because it went on forever like the scrubland, but it had caves and cliffs and crags and definition.

She put her hand on my head. "Where's your scarf?"

"I lost it in my dream. The wind blew it away. Can I have one of yours?"

"You put it on the windowsill and left the window open, you mean. That was very clumsy."

I scowled. That wasn't what I meant.

She sighed. "Now I have to buy another."

"I'm sorry."

"If we were in the mountains, I would invite a woman to dinner and she would make you a good scarf."

"I'll go to the mountain in my dream and get a scarf."

She shook her head and I snuck guiltily out of the house with her green scarf that showed the coils of my hair underneath. I took my mule to the hill. Maybe I'd run away to the mountain to get another scarf. That was a bad thought, because I lay down in the heather on the hill and stood up hours away, the squat village like rocks among the yellow bushes. But the mountain was still far away, just a tear in the horizon.

My mule snorted as I mounted up. It took us a long time to get back. At the edge of town, a woman looked at us out her window and came out around the front of her house. I tried to turn away, but she came out too fast.

"Good evening," she said. It was the teacher who wanted to take me to school. "Not many people around here have mules." She leaned down and scratched my mule's jaw. "I hear they're not very cleanly."

I held tight to my mule's mane. "They're tenacious. She loves me and takes me where I want."

The woman flicked her fingers like she was dislodging dust and gnats from under her nails. She smelled like fish. "Are you from around here?"

I wanted to say yes. It was my town and I knew it very well. "No."

"Where are you going?"

"I'm riding through."

She smiled, her eyes pinching. "Haven't we met before? I remember. You said you were riding through then too."

"I ride through a lot."

"Mosi's mother wears a scarf like that."

"She got it from my mother. My mother makes these scarves. No one else makes them like this." I remembered then that my aunt had bought the scarf in town and flushed with fear.

The teacher locked her fingers together. "Perhaps you'd like to come in for supper."

I shook my head.

21

"I insist. You must be hungry. I have red tea, fresh from the fields, and sole fillet with mint."

"I don't like fish."

"You don't know how good it is. This is what happens, when you grow up on birds. Everything else scares you. You're flighty."

"I have to get where I'm going." I dug my heels into my mule's side, jerking her away from the woman. The woman watched me go, her stance trim and disappointed.

I rushed inside when I got to the house. It was dark and the walls stretched away into a terrifying vastness. It was like they weren't there at all. I climbed into bed with Mosi. She didn't like me holding her at night, but I squeezed up against her, staring until I found all the corners in the room.

It isn't my dream. Or I think it's not. The sands unravels behind me and I stand on the ocean shore. The water goes on forever, dizzying. It's unfair that I should find the ocean, when I can't find the mountain.

A woman stops beside me and jams her fork into the sand. She takes a deep and satisfied breath. *Ahhh*, she breathes.

"I'll send the ocean away," I say.

She gazes up, the skin crinkling around her eyes. "This is home, sweetheart."

I shake my head hard.

Her coat is like stone. "If your cousin goes to the ocean, you could go to school with her," she says. "Then you wouldn't miss her."

"But I would miss my aunt."

"If you were in a schoolhouse all day, you would be better. You would always sit in the same seat and know where you should be. And there's a drawer in the desk for you to keep your things."

"Can I lock it?" I've never had a thing before that I could lock.

"Good students can keep locked boxes inside their desk. If you went to school, you could bring your friends to the house and say, 'This is my home. This is where I live.' "

I like the idea. Then I could tell the teacher I live here and I'm growing into the shape of my house. "What about the mountain?"

Tsk, a woman says, *tsk*. "The mountain is a bad place to live. It's dangerous. There are no houses, so everything is unstable."

"Oupa lives in a big tent. My aunt says that's his house." But I don't feel very certain about it.

I try to imagine Oupa on the waves, kneeling in a boat, crouched on a reed mat with the sea birds and the white seashells. But it's impossible. My dream cracks around my waist, nearly breaking in half with the impossibility of it. Oupa can't come here, not ever. If he saw me now, he'd say I was the wrong shape and he couldn't teach me. I hold onto a woman's coat, wanting to step into the black recesses that are like tall walls, so that I don't crack all the way through.

My aunt stood with her hands hovering over the open cupboards. She stared at the lemons and the pepper and the barley flour. Her hands rested on a tin of red tea leaves, which she bought in the summer and said were very expensive. Her hands slipped to the dried mutton and salted pheasant.

I watched her from the doorway, my toes up against the lintel.

"If only I had a scrap of fish," she muttered.

Goosebumps ran up and down my arms and I put my hand on the doorframe so I wouldn't find myself a great distance away. "Should I kill a chicken?"

Her hands scrunched, fingers folding up tight against her palm. "Yes."

I killed a chicken outside and plucked the feathers, putting them in my pocket for pillows. Mosi came and crouched nearby, squinting. Her hair tumbled down her back, whipping over her mouth.

"My teacher's coming for dinner," she said. "Are you going to hide in the cupboard?"

I shrugged, even though I didn't want to go into the cupboard. There was a stiffness in my throat and I was afraid if I went in there, I would cry. It wasn't a good shape.

"How do you do that?" she asked

"Nana taught me." She died when I was young, but I remembered plucking birds was important. I held out the chicken and Mosi crept forward. I showed her how to grasp the feather so she wouldn't tear the skin.

When Mosi's teacher came, I didn't go to the cupboard. I sat in the closet under the stairs where I could look through a crack in the panels, and sucked on my fingers. If I decided I liked the teacher, maybe I could come out. The teacher came in a flower printed skirt, which flapped against her knees. She smiled and took my aunt's hand with only her fingers.

"I hope you don't mind," she said. "I brought a little something for dinner. I came home early today and I had extra time. I thought, wouldn't it be nice if I brought something to share?"

My aunt nodded, small. She picked up the chicken, which we'd cooked into a thick stew with bay leaves.

"Oh, no. I didn't mean to supplant your own meal." But she let my aunt take the stew away, and replaced it with her own plate. It was a fish of some sort, large and white and stuffed with sweet-smelling pears and apples. It smelled good.

The teacher insisted everyone wash their hands in the sink, scrubbing between their fingers before they ate. Everyone sat very quietly. My aunt didn't eat with a fork usually and she grasped the handle with her whole hand. The teacher held the fork with the ends of her fingers so that it dipped gracefully. She smiled at Mosi, who blushed and looked very proud. It made me jealous.

"Your daughter is a wonderful student," the teacher said.

My aunt nodded.

"You mustn't be concerned that I'm coming with bad news." She spoke with her hands, holding them out like she hoped my aunt would grasp them warmly. "Don't look so worried. I don't have one bad thing to say about her."

Mosi grinned at her mother, who didn't look at her. "Yesterday," Mosi said, "We learned about the new houses they're building on the coast to withstand the flooding."

Her teacher smiled encouragingly. I imagined building a small house out of seashells and the teacher looking at me like that. Maybe I could learn good things at the school and then grow into the shape of the house instead of its cupboards and closets.

"I'm very excited," the teacher said. "You see, there's a lovely boarding school by the seashore. Very safe, of course, and not too near the water. I went to visit last month. It's cleaned every day and the students can play on the beach. There's

27

fresh fish in the morning and once a week they go fishing."

My aunt chewed fast, like she was trying to swallow before the teacher could finish speaking. But the fish went back and forth in her mouth and she couldn't seem to swallow.

The teacher beamed. "We'd like to send your daughter there."

My aunt coughed, spitting up a half-chewed piece of bone and fish.

The teacher jumped. I did too.

"I'm sorry," my aunt said. As if to remedy her fault, she cut off another piece of fish and put it in her mouth.

"That is to say," the teacher said, her hand on her chest, "all the students will be going there, eventually. But we'd like to send your daughter sooner."

"Mama, I have to go," Mosi said, hopping up onto her knees. A shock of horror went through me.

My aunt waved her back and Mosi slid down on her seat. When my aunt swallowed, it was like something huge was going down her throat, bulging the skin tight.

The teacher put out her hand. "I know it'll be hard for your daughter to move so far away. But you can visit. Or you can move to the shore, even. We'll help you buy a house and find a job, maybe skinning fish or somesuch."

"Yes, mama," Mosi said. "Come live with me."

My aunt stared at her daughter, her eyes wide and confused. "I've lived in this house my whole life."

"Your daughter told me that your father came down the mountain as a young man. Wouldn't it be following in his footsteps to move to the ocean?"

My aunt blinked at her. It was as if the woman had slipped her father under her nails like slivers of wood. "I could see Mosi then?"

I put my face against the panel, the wood smell strong in my nose. I thought of yelling to her that she couldn't go because then I would be alone. My body would spill over the scrubland and I'd vanish.

"Of course. It is a boarding school, so she'll sleep over. But she can visit you on the weekend, if she chooses."

My aunt set aside her fork. "I don't see any reason why she should go earlier than the other students."

Mosi gripped her fork, bits of fish still caught on the tines. "Don't you think I'm a good student?"

"Of course you're a good student," my aunt mumbled.

"Your daughter will benefit by going early. It's a better school."

"I don't want her to go."

The teacher folded her fingers together, poised over her fork. "There's another thing." She glanced around the house, frowning at the rugs on the walls, the sunflower seed oil on the counter, the unwashed dishes. I shrunk back into the closet. "Your niece."

"She doesn't live here," my aunt said automatically.

The teacher sighed, her shoulders heaving up in exasperation. "We've played this ruse for a long time. We've let you get away with it and we shouldn't have. We know your niece lives here, and it's illegal to keep her from school."

Mosi glanced at the stairs and squeezed down in her chair, shoving fish into her mouth. I was terrified that the teacher would stand up and thrust her hand into the closet and drag me to school right now. I wouldn't go to school if they meant to send me to the ocean.

"The next semester starts with the rainy season. Mosi will go to the school on the shore and your niece will start school here. It'll be better for everyone."

My aunt shook her head, but said nothing. The teacher wiped her mouth and popped up cheerily. "Thank you so much for supper. Please, keep what's left of the fish. It's my gift to you."

When she was gone, my aunt slid down until her head sunk into her arms. Mosi sat still, staring at her mother collapsed across the table. I leaned against the closet door, the doorknob pushing painfully into my hip, needing someone to say it wasn't true. Mosi stood, clenching her hands opened and closed, and left the room.

In my dream, the wind ripples the ocean waves, hushes, holds still. But then the tide gushes up the beach, washing over my knees, and I slosh out with the water, tumbling over the waves. I'm drowning. I catch my throat in my hands and bubbles pour of my mouth. There's nothing here to hold me. I spill until I am so big and thin that it's like I'm nothing at all.

I got up early so Mosi couldn't leave for the ocean without talking to me. My tongue was thick with salt. My aunt stayed inside, putting chicken stew into small pots sealed with leather caps. She moved slowly, stopping often to stare out the window. Mosi sat outside on her suitcase, rubbing her nose red.

"Do you think it'll be cold?" she said. "What if my sweater is too thin?"

"Wear a scarf over your hair." I scuffed my heels in the dirt.

"It's not allowed at the new school."

But she wore a scarf now, which she hadn't done in months. It tucked neatly under her sweater collar, crafted into a perfect curve against her back.

"You could wear it if you weren't being stupid and going," I said.

She stiffened. "I have to go."

I wrinkled my nose at the road winding toward the school and the car that would come for her. "I've never slept alone before."

"They'll make you go too."

I scratched my wrists and rammed my toes against the step. "Nana would be angry."

"Nana's dead."

I shoved her and she grabbed my hand, holding tight to my wrist. She looked at me and squeezed and squeezed. "Ow," I said. But she didn't let go, just kept squeezing until my wrist cramped. "Ow!" I shouted, jerking away.

She clasped her hands and stared down at her lap. "I wish you'd come."

"No. I hate the ocean. I hate it."

She buffed the side of her shoe with her wrist. "You've never seen it."

"I want to go to the mountains."

"What if there's no one left there anymore?"

I pushed my heels hard against the step. "They're still there. They'll teach me how to set up a tent and whenever I'm afraid of how big everything is, I'll set up my tent and sit inside."

Under her breath, like she was saying something forbidden, she asked, "Can you dream about the ocean and visit me?"

The sky spun and I had to sit down. I put my arm around her. "Yes."

She flushed and straightened her cuffs. "I'll write letters."

The door rattled and banged, catching on the frame as my aunt came out with a pot for lunch. Mosi put it in her bag. My aunt crouched behind us and fiddled with Mosi's scarf.

"What if we ran into the mountains like me and my grandmother did, when I was a girl?" my aunt said, very quiet.

I squeezed my hands shut. I wanted that very much. But my aunt would never go.

Mosi patted her bag, checking that everything was there. Then she stood, brushed off her uniform, and grabbed her mother around the waist. She held so tight her mother gasped and her hand fluttered indecisively over Mosi's back.

Then the car came and she left us standing alone on the stoop.

I sit in the surf, water dripping down my back and my clothes soaked through. When I twist out my hair, a river spills away. The ocean waves beat against my chest. I'm so angry I want to cry. All the ocean does is take people away. Nana wouldn't have gone. She knew the mountain was where she should be and was happy in her tent. Why couldn't a tent be a house? It was as much a house as anything.

The mud sticks and scrapes when I stand. But when I'm on my feet, I see something caught on the waves. I run to it and when I snatch it up, it's my scarf, the one I lost in my other dream. I wring it out and bind it over my hair.

In the morning, it started to rain. As I tucked my hair behind my scarf, I realized it was the scarf I found in my dream. I went into the kitchen and found my aunt opening drawers loudly. She hadn't slept. I'd heard her moving around all night, stacking plates and pouring water and then sitting at the table, the chair creaking when she shifted.

"You'll go to school today," she said.

I shook my head.

She rubbed her face, holding herself up on the counter with her left hand. "You have to go. I'll be arrested if you stay here."

"I'm going to be a buzzard!"

She stared down at her hand. "I'll still tell you stories about Oupa in the evening.

We'll sit outside and look for his home in the clouds."

"They'll send me to the ocean." My arms flopped over the table like awful cooked fish. "I went to the ocean in my dream and I drowned."

Her hands went over the sink, rubbing and rubbing so it said *shush, shush*. "You didn't go anywhere. You just dreamed about it because you were thinking about the ocean."

"I found my scarf in my dream last night." I held up the scarf to show it was true.

She snapped her hands together. "You lost it under the bed or stuffed it into the bottom of your chest."

"No. Nana went places in her dreams."

"No she didn't. It was a good story. She couldn't do that." She grabbed a plate and set it down in front of me. Honey pooled over yesterday's bread.

I stared at her as she sat down and started eating. She didn't look at me. The corners of her mouth were firm and angry. I didn't understand how she could say that about Nana. It was the most impossible thing she'd ever said.

"You can't travel places in your dreams," she said.

I knocked against the walls. I spilled out the open door and the window. I drowned in the arid air.

I didn't finish breakfast. I packed lunch and extra food because I'd always eaten when I wanted and I was terrified of being told I could only eat at a certain time. Outside, through the drizzle, I searched for Oupa's circle tent in the clouds. It began to rain so hard the world turned grey and brown. My scarf plastered to my hair. I splashed through water, looking for my mule. Everything vanished into the downpour.

The house was dim and hazy. All the lamps were out and it was floating at sea, vast and empty. My heels sank into the mud and I was floating too. My skin crawled. The house was a bad shape. If I went in it again, it would crush me with its twisted rooms and slippery stairs and bent doorways. It was the wrong shape.

In the mountains, I would find a cave and the cave would hold me until the rains passed.

When I found my mule, I packed the saddlebags and mounted quickly, urging her on to the slippery road. The town was blue, vanishing in the coming tide. I could be anywhere, or nowhere. Water ran down my back and chest and my pants stuck to my thighs. My aunt would stay here forever, drifting aimlessly. I watched a buzzard fly under the clouds, its feathers black with rain. It was going toward the mountain. When it got there, people might see it and then tell how Oupa and Buzzard became friends. They would tell it inside their tents and they wouldn't mind that the walls flapped in the storm, because that was the shape they'd grown into. If I were there, I'd grow into that shape too, instead of a rigid, crooked house.

I pulled my mule around, digging my heels so hard into her sides that she leapt. She landed at a gallop and we pounded out of town.

"We'll go to the mountains," I said into her ear, mud from her hooves splashing against my shins. "Our family lived at the rim of the mountain and they weren't hard to find. Oupa will teach me to be persistent like Buzzard and strong like Nana. I'll sit in a tent and grow into it and it'll be my home. I think maybe tents aren't houses, but they can still be homes."

In the evening, the rain cleared. The mountains were white and red slips on the horizon, cutting out a small space for themselves in the sky. By morning they were bigger than even the women with their forks, and I could see smoke from cook fires. I imagined Oupa when he first came to the mountain, watching in wonder as Buzzard flew up and up and up and yet never seemed to reach the top. When Oupa finally reached the foothills, he put his hips and knees against the mountain crags and found that he fit. I reached the mountain that evening and as we went up the rocky paths, the peaks rose up like tents.

See Sarah McGill's story "A Yellow Landscape" online at Metaphorosis.
If you liked it, leave a comment. Authors love that!
Remember to subscribe to our e-mail updates so you'll know when new stories are posted.

About the story

I wrote "A Yellow Landscape" after reading Gaston Bachelard's *The Poetics of Space*, which is a series of gorgeous essays on physical space in poetry. I was caught by his descriptions of a house as a very physical and yet deeply symbolic shell around the self. The protagonist of "A Yellow Landscape" moves around a house that is not her house, in search of a place inside it. It's her home, so she should have grown into its shape, but it isn't and she hasn't.

From that restlessness it was inevitable for her to explore other types of houses – shells, tents, mountains. Is a tent a house? I think so, but not everyone would agree. A tent has a built-in instability, a formlessness, and while hierarchy and designated spaces certainly exist, there aren't as many thresholds and barriers such as stairs or cabinets to be breached. So intimacy comes more quickly. Yet a tent isn't shapeless. That dynamic and difference was something I wanted to explore.

The word 'vast,' a dream-like, endless word, also caught my imagination and created my protagonist's dream landscape. The artwork of Akiya Kageichi had a hand in her dreams as well, especially the color and size of them. They are colorful, yet muted, and shift frequently between rigidity and fluidity. I hope you go searching for his work yourself. It's gorgeous and intricate and vast.

A question for the author

Q: Do you live near where you were born? Have you traveled much?

A: I generally live far away from the Twin Cities where I was born – the furthest away was New Zealand. Most recently, over the summer I lived in northern Minnesota, which was closer to Canada than really anything else. I do travel quite a lot. The whole family picked up and moved to New Zealand for six months when I was a sophomore in high school. At the time *High School Musical* was very popular and I spent a lot of time explaining that that wasn't really an accurate representation of American high school or America in general. I also decided I didn't like wearing a uniform, even if it was a kilt. But they do have golden kiwis, which are better than regular kiwis and one day I'll go back, if only to eat golden kiwis again.

About the author

Sarah McGill has been a tour guide in Ohio, a student in New Zealand, a stage manager in New York, and a canoe outfitter in Minnesota. Her favorite time and place is post-revolution France at the height of the Death Cabarets through the end of the Grand Guignol, mostly because the bohemians really did walk their alligators in the rose gardens and pretend hydropathes were Canadian animals whose feet were made into drinking glasses. She wishes she knew how to sail and had more cats.

Sarahmcgillwrites.com, @sarahmcgillwrit

Forever and a Life

Daniel Roy

Transcripts of Mayfly interviews by Dr. Leanne Jansen.

Sarah al-Awqati (childhood friend): "Fuck forever." Yup, I was right in front of the stage when she first said that. I can say "she," right?

Interviewer: Sure, if you like.

Al-Awqati: She was smoking a cig on stage when she said it. Ever seen those? Little paper sticks that smelled like burnt grass. Anyway: [Al-Awqati inhales an imaginary cig, then exhales invisible smoke as she speaks.] "Fuck forever." Like that.

Esra Agnarsson (Mayfly survivor):
You asked if Sylvia Castro believed it.
Look, there's no denying that a few of us
thought it was an act, but me... Castro
was so much larger than life, y'know? I
could tell she meant it. She wanted to
punch immortality in the balls.

Interviewer: Do you think she acted
out of anger against the Autocracy?

Agnarsson: What? Oh, no no no. Of
course not.

*Recorded at the Olivia Castro Center of the
Arts on the fiftieth anniversary of Sylvia
Castro's death.*

[Polite applause.]

Olivia Castro: Freedom. That's what
my grandson wanted, not just for himself
but for each and every one of us. The
freedom to *choose* to be immortal, to
embrace this great gift that the Autocracy,
praise be, has made possible.

Now, you might wonder who in their
right mind would choose *not* to live
forever. That's okay, I do too, sometimes.
[Laughter.] It's tempting to look down on
those poor souls who would rather live
short, brutish lives than shine like a

beacon through the ages with us. Some historians look back on the life of Sylvain Castro and find all sorts of pathologies and mental defects that led him down this path.

But I know my grandson. I bounced him on my lap when he was just a little boy. Whatever mental state led him to reject immortality, it doesn't diminish the importance of his grand idea. It doesn't negate the significance of his contribution.

Each of us here is alive because we *want* it. The Autocracy is our *choice*. This is our freedom, and we have Sylvain Castro to thank for reminding us. Thank you, Sylvain. And praise the Autocracy for keeping us safe through the centuries to come!

[Sustained applause.]

[Wang Xian-zhi frowns as he listens to the recording of Olivia Castro's speech.]

Wang Xian-zhi (Mayfly survivor, *Rotting Corpse* drummer): Yeah, Olivia's full of shit. [Laughter.]

Interviewer: Why do you say that?

Wang: Sylvain—*Sylvia*. Sylvia didn't do all this to give us a choice, man. She hated immortality, plain and simple. She hated that we all gave up on our freedom because we were afraid of what might happen three hundred years down the line. What Olivia talks about isn't a choice at all. "Be young and healthy forever barring traumatic injury, or die a slow, agonizing death as your body breaks down." Who in hell would choose the latter?

Olivia's notion of freedom is like setting a cage on the edge of a cliff and opening the door. No one in their right mind would step out.

Now back before Sylvia, that door wasn't even open. Then came the attacks in '89—

Interviewer: The London Underground gas attacks that claimed the immortality of three hundred and fifty-seven victims.

Wang: Right, right. Back then, Sylvia and I were getting the band started on the Montreal music scene, and we'd play these songs that were critical of the Autocracy, right? So even though we had nothing to do with '89, the Secret Police had their eye on us. And the Secret Police had developed, like, this vaccine that could switch off your immortality. The

Mayfly Shot, you know about it! They used it to threaten us.

Interviewer: Threaten you how?

Wang: Like, they'd rough us up pretty bad, then while a nurse tends to you, bam! They'd stab you with a syringe and let you think you just got the Mayfly Shot. Rattle our nerves. Shit, it worked.

Interviewer: Did you believe it at the time? That they had an immortality vaccine?

Wang: We didn't know for sure, but we were scared. I begged Sylvia to take it down a notch with the anti-Autocracy lyrics and speeches, but, man, she just didn't care. "Relax, Wangie!" she'd say, and she'd laugh that deep laugh of hers, like life was just a big joke. Then one day she showed up at practice and she had the syringe.

Video footage seized from Wang's personal collection, on lease from Montreal's Self-Enforcement Agency.

[The grainy, amateur video is shot in a loft in Downtown Montreal. It focuses on Sylvia Castro, unaware she's being filmed, as she bounces a small syringe on her knuckles, staring into the distance. At the back of the shot, someone is tuning an electric guitar.]

Wang Xian-zhi (offscreen, filming): What you got there, Syl?

[Sylvia looks up. Her long hair and painted face make her look unmistakably feminine. She twirls the syringe like a drumstick, and grins at the camera.]

Sylvia Castro: Mayfly Shot. Want a go?

Wang: Bullshit, man, that's totally mouthwash.

Sylvia: You think? Let's find out!

[Sylvia places the syringe against her arm, smiling wide.]

Wang: Hey. Hey! Sylvia! Take it easy, man!

[Sylvia pockets the syringe, seemingly pleased with Wang's reaction.]

Sylvia: Don't worry, I'm not gonna waste this for a documentary that no one's ever gonna watch.

Wang: Anything else you wanna say to the camera, since nobody's watching this?

Sylvia: [Cheerfully.] Fuck the Autocracy!

Esra Agnarsson (off-screen): Hey! Not cool.

Sylvia: See, Wangie? That's what I'm talking about. Eternal life has turned us all into wimps, man. We used to know better! "Better to burn out than to fade away."

Wang: Here we go—

Sylvia: You know I'm right. We've given up our freedoms because we're scared of what might happen a thousand years from now! It's fucked up.

Esra (off-screen): Living beats dying.

Sylvia: Does it? Maybe dying is the only way to live.

Wang: Okay. I'm turning this off.

[The video ends.]

Interviewer: State your name and occupation, please.

Doctor Gerald Stone: Doctor Gerald Stone, Mayfly Program Director.

Interviewer: What was your position at the time Castro was admitted?

Stone: I was the director of the Melody Dementia Care Center in Stark, New Hampshire. It wasn't devoted to Mayflies back then.

Interviewer: So Castro was considered mentally unsound when he—

Stone: She.

Interviewer: Yes, of course. I'm just careful around officials when it comes to Castro's... That is...

Stone: I'm a medical practitioner, Miss, not a politician.

Interviewer: Is this why you allowed Sylvia and the others freedom around the facilities?

Stone: It was a sound medical practice. By taking the vaccine, they had inflicted grievous self-harm. They condemned themselves to a slow, life-long death.

I just did what was right by them, as my patients. I gave them an environment where they could be themselves. Who cared about the Autocracy's official party line if these people were gonna die sixty, eighty years later? It was the humane thing to do. That's all.

Interviewer: Why do you think Sylvia Castro took the Mayfly Shot? Was it an act of suicide or rebellion?

Stone: Yes.

Attached: picture of Rotting Corpse *in concert in the Melody community hall in January '91.*

Description: Sylvia Castro, wearing a white tank top and frilly camouflage skirt over ripped fishnets, holds her fist up at a crowd of patients. The crowd, excited by the performance, hold up their fists in response. Behind Sylvia, to the right of the frame, is Wang Xian-zhi.

Esra Agnarsson (Mayfly survivor): Word got around. The way the rumors put it, Sylvia was running the asylum, like, literally. They put on punk performances almost every night. *Rotting Corpse*, but also a few others that had followed Sylvia's example and taken the shot, like *Short Flight* and *Kick the System*. There were rumors of drugs and sex, y'know. And other stuff.

Nabila Safar (Mayfly survivor): We couldn't believe it. Sylvia had spoken against the Autocracy, and now she was in some sort of utopian center where she played music and got to be a girl and shit! Like Esra said… Word got around.

Agnarsson: Some of us got hold of the Mayfly Shot. I asked Sylvia's friends, and someone put me in touch. Friend of a friend kinda deal. They didn't even charge me for it... They were just thrilled to give them out. All you had to do was take it, and you'd get sent to Melody.

Interviewer: Did you realize you were gonna die if you took the vaccine?

Agnarsson: Well, yeah. But not right away, know what I mean? It just didn't feel real. Eighty years isn't a long time, but it's long enough that you don't have to think about it too much. Of course, I hadn't realized I'd get progressively older, y'know? I thought I'd stay twenty until I turned ninety, then bam, old woman.

Safar: I didn't really think about it at the time, to be honest. I thought someone would find a way to reverse the vaccine.

Agnarsson: Well, they did, but not before... [Agnarsson motions to her wrinkled face.]

Safar: Yeah.

Interviewer: What were you told when you got to the center?

Agnarsson: The medical staff called us "Mayflies." They said they wanted us happy in the time we had left, that this was a safe space. I remember one nurse— Jenny, I think her name was. She did my check-in, and near the end she took my hand and just... teared up. She couldn't speak for a while.

Interviewer: What about you, Sarah? Why didn't you take the shot?

Sarah al-Awqadi (childhood friend): Me? [Nervous laughter.] I was scared, what do you think? I mean, I thought about it. I even got my own shot. I sat in my room one night and put the tip of the syringe to my arm... I must have spent an hour just poking at my skin with it. But I... I couldn't go through with it. I just couldn't.

Interviewer: Do you regret not doing it?

Al-Awqadi: Well, no, I... [Long pause.] No.

Jenny Preston (Melody nurse): I didn't like their music. To call it "music" is charitable, to be honest. It was mostly yelling and mindless strumming on antique instruments. I got one of those old music files the Mayflies passed around, stuff like *Sex Pistols* and *Dead Kennedys*. First time I heard them, I thought the file was corrupted.

Interviewer: Were you aware that recordings were being smuggled out?

Preston: Not at first. When the Mayfly Riots started, though, there was no doubt where the rioters out there were getting their inspiration. Doctor Stone put security measures in place, but it didn't do any good. I'm pretty sure it was one of the orderlies smuggling out the recordings. We never found out who.

Interviewer: Stone didn't put a stop to the shows even then?

Preston: Well, the damage was already done. Besides, Doctor Stone would never let politics influence his medical practice. The only thing he cared about was the well-being of his patients, and it was clear they were happier this way.

Interviewer: One of the Mayflies has testified under oath that you were the one smuggling the tapes out.

Preston: Hmm.

Interviewer: You don't dispute it?

Preston: Probably someone out to get me. Like I said, the music was garbage.

James Maarten (rioter): Everybody in the movement saw the recordings. Sylvia and the others, they looked so damn *free*! No disciplinary circles, no loyalty broadcasts, no Secret Police. It made us question whether immortality was really worth it. We all understood you can't have a society of immortals without absolute rule of law, of course, but still, the question itself bugged the hell out of us.

Castro's choice meant that things could be different. None of us wanted to die, not really. I mean, the Mayfly Shot was outlawed at this point, but it was still available if you knew the right people. And sure, some in the movement ended up in Melody, but for most of us, it wasn't immortality that was the problem.

Interviewer: What was the problem, then?

Maarten: I, uh... [Nervous laugh.]

Interviewer: Can I show you a video? [Maarten shrugs.]

Video attached: Maarten speech in September '82. He is standing in front of a small crowd in Central Park, holding up his fist and speaking in a megaphone being held by a woman with her face out of frame.

Maarten (in video): *We offered them peace, and they answered with crowd control drones! We held out our hand and they slapped it with nightsticks! You know why, right?* [Incoherent whooping.] *Yeah,*

I'll tell you why! Because violence is the only language the Autocracy understands. [Boos.] *Violence is the only way they know!*

Maarten: Ah... [Pause.] Look, we weren't thinking straight... I never meant for the riots to happen. Those were fringe elements of the movement. Extremists.

Interviewer: You didn't mean what you said about the Autocracy?

Maarten: [Agitated.] No. No, of course not!

Interviewer: Tell me about your grandson.

Olivia Castro (grandmother of Sylvia Castro): He is a hero to us all. His thirst for freedom has inspired a new generation to not only embrace immortality and its infinite rewards, but also appreciate what it means by giving us a vision of the alternative. It helped a new generation understand the need for the Autocracy.

Interviewer: And as a person? Tell me how he was growing up.

Castro: Oh, well, what is there to tell? He was a happy little boy. Full of life and energy, always laughing and running around. That's what surprised me when I heard he took the Mayfly Shot... He always seemed to love life so much.

Interviewer: Were there early signs of his madness?

Castro: Yeah. Yeah, sure.

Interviewer: Can you talk about those?

Castro: Well, for one he liked girl clothes. And playing with dolls. Once his mom tried to convince him to play with trucks and took his dolls away, but he just put the trucks to bed and told them bedtime stories. [Laughter.]

Interviewer: Do you think this has something to do with his decision to take the shot?

Castro: No.

Interviewer: Perhaps his gender dysphoria caused him a great deal of stress... Do you think it's possible that—

Castro: I thought you were writing a history of the Mayflies? Is this line of questioning sanctioned by your university's monitors?

Interviewer: I mean no dis—

Castro: Well, I resent your implication that Sylvain's parents and I failed him as caretakers.

Interviewer: That's not what I'm saying at all.

[Long pause.]

Castro: Oh my, look at the time. My apologies, but I have to prepare for a meeting.

Interviewer: Describe Sylvia Castro in the last days.

Wang Xian-zhi: In public or in private? In public she was her old self, like, boisterous, didn't give a shit about authority. She'd say things just to rile you up, then laugh with her mouth open and her head thrown back, like she just heard the funniest joke. She'd party harder than any of us, even when she was stuck in bed. One time she had us pour vodka directly into her saline bag!

Interviewer: And in private?

Wang: Well, she was... quieter. She'd watch us from her bed with that big grin of hers, like she wanted to make sure everyone had a good time. But when she figured no one was looking, she'd get that look in her eyes.

Interviewer: That look?

Wang: You know, man. Like she couldn't wait for this shit to be over.

Interviewer: You were one of the first rioters to enter Melody, correct?

Herbert Gilmore (rioter): I was an activist, not a rioter. But yeah.

Interviewer: Why were you and other activists trying to enter the center?

Gilmore: The movement was losing steam. The media was portraying us as looters and madmen, so we knew we had to do something big. And the Mayflies, well, they had started all of this, right? We figured they could help. Especially Sylvia.

Interviewer: Were the Mayflies what you expected?

Gilmore: Not at all. I mean, I've seen pictures of old people from ancient times, I know what they're like. They don't feel real, though, know what I mean? You see all those wrinkles... You don't realize they're actual *grooves*. And some of the Mayflies didn't seem entirely lucid, either. And they moved so slow, like frozen bugs...

Interviewer: Tell me what it was like seeing the Mayflies for the first time in sixty years.

Gilmore: The Melody staff had moved them to the community hall because the Autocracy had warned them we were coming. We, well... We convinced the staff to let us talk to them. When I opened the door... It's the smell I noticed first. It was an *animal* smell, like when you get a whiff of a carcass by the side of the road, right? Except... It came from living human beings.

Interviewer: How did the Mayflies react?

Gilmore: They were... Honestly, they were relieved to see us. A bunch of them were crying. They thought we had come to save them.

Interviewer: Save them from what?

Gilmore: Yeah, well. That's the question that keeps me up at night.

Video footage seized from Wang's personal collection, on lease from Montreal's Self-Enforcement Agency.

[The video is shot at the Mayfly Center during the break-in, and shows Sylvia, in bed, surrounded by monitors and hooked up to a dialysis machine. Her cheekbones jut through the parchment-like skin of her face.]

Wang Xian-zhi (offscreen, filming): Sylvia! We gotta go! The protestors have broken in. They're here for us!

[Sylvia half-opens her eyes.]

Sylvia: Tell them they're too late.

Wang: C'mon, Syl. They say they can reverse the Mayfly Shot. We don't have to die anymore, man!

[Sylvia, her eyes now fully open, stares in silent anger at Wang.]

Wang: You're a legend out there, Sylvia! They need a leader.

Sylvia: [Tired chuckle.] Please. I can't even piss by myself anymore. [Long silence.] No... Better they think I went out rocking with my tits out and a cig in my mouth.

Wang: [Choking back tears.] C'mon, Syl. You can't die. Not you.

[Sylvia attempts to laugh, but all she manages is a wheeze. Still, in that moment, she looks something like her old self.]

Sylvia: Of course I can. I've been dying my whole life.

See Daniel Roy's story "Forever and a Life"
online at Metaphorosis.
If you liked it, leave a comment. Authors love
that!
Remember to subscribe to our e-mail updates so
you'll know when new stories are posted.

About the story

One of the paradoxes of aging is that the less life we have left ahead of us, the more we obsess about extending this time. Death-defying acts of rebellion have almost always been led by the young, after all. It led to me wonder: how fearful of death could someone be if they could theoretically live forever? What would they be willing to sacrifice in exchange for eternity? And what would rebellion look like in such a world?

A few years ago, I stumbled upon a story about youth in 1980s Cuba who willingly injected themselves with HIV to protest their treatment under Castro. I had found the perfect allegory for the struggle between self-preservation and the creative destruction of rebellion. What's more "punk rock" than kicking eternity in the teeth? What kind of people could willingly walk away from life itself? What could they possibly hope to accomplish by doing so?

This story felt perfect for an oral history format, as I wanted to tell the story of Sylvia Castro in her full contradictions. I didn't seek to cast a crude light on her psyche as much as explore the shadows she cast across the rest of the world. This was not a big story about wars and revolutions: I wanted to tell the story of one meaningful life, and the ripples that life could cast across society.

As I explored this vision of Sylvia through my writing, I was struck by how much it paralleled the plight of many of the people I know who are transgender, and how they have to fight for the utmost basic right to even exist. Sylvia already lived in my mind as a fully-formed character at this point, so I felt confident I could write her as a full-fledged character that happened to be trans. And so, with humble apologies to my trans brothers and sisters, I borrowed some of their courage and their unflinching sense of self in the face of adversity to lend it to Sylvia as she struggled for a life well lived.

A question for the author

Q: What's better: writing or having written?

A: People love to rave about the blissful process of writing, but let me tell you... Having written beats writing, no contest.

Writing is the messy act of giving birth: I bare my guts on the computer screen, and in the thick of this bloody, miraculous, godawful process, there is no way to know if either I or my creation will ever emerge whole. The hope keeps me going: that one day, I will have written, and that this small, bloody corner of my soul will know a modicum of peace before the renewed siren call of writing rises once more.

But having written, ah, now there's the blissful part. My words are finally free to reach others and germinate their own imaginations. Perhaps these people will hate it, but never as much as I did writing and revising it; or perhaps they will fall in love with my story, but never as fiercely nor as desperately as I.

There's a supreme vitality to writing, and there is no having written without the writing part. But the reward of writing, for me, is found in having written, in watching my creation go forth into the world, having left the bruised mess of my mind behind for greener pastures.

About the author

Daniel Roy is a Canadian video game narrative writer, slow traveler, and backpack foodie. Originally from Montreal, he has also lived in China, Thailand, India, and South Korea. He is currently based in Sofia, Bulgaria.

www.onebluepixel.net, @1bluepixel

With Eyes Half Open

Frances Pauli

The circus smelled of magic, of popcorn, dung, and cotton candy. Miranda squinted as she entered, just like the book suggested. She followed the crowd through the gate, then slipped between the wagons, searching for something only half open eyes could see.

Magic dwells in the halfway places, in the between times and the long shadows that cannot be perceived with the eyes wide.

She'd borrowed the book without asking, the one with gold designs on the cover and a layer of dust marred only by her aunt's knobby fingerprints. Miranda had read the bits of it that she could understand, cradling the tome underneath the covers in the late hours while her aunt slept.

That was how she knew the jugglers were only ordinary jugglers. It was how she knew the strong man and his dumbbells were fake. Miranda squinted at them all and found only disappointment.

Until she saw the bear.

He lay against the back of his cage, striped with the shadows of iron bars and wearing a pill box hat on his wide head. When Miranda squinted at the bear, his edges shifted. The dense, cinnamon fur melted and smoothed. *Inside* the bear, a man hid. Inside the cage, he stared at her with soft, brown eyes.

Miranda stepped closer, whispered. "I think you're more than just a bear."

"Careful." The growling voice might have come from ursine lips, except the sound was behind her.

She turned and faced the ringmaster, complete with top hat, spangled shirt, and snake-slender whip.

"You seem to have wandered off track, my dear." The ringmaster's eyes flashed crystal clear. "Don't want to get too close to old Boris. He's a bit cranky."

"I got separated." Miranda's feet shuffled as she walked away from the cage, but she couldn't resist a glance back over one shoulder.

Boris sat with his big rear paws stuck out in front of him, each tipped with gleaming sickle claws. The hat leaned at an angle on his tilted head, and when Miranda's gaze met those brown eyes, the bear's muzzle dipped forward. Secretly, through squinting eyes, she saw Boris nodding to her.

More than just a bear.

"Let me show you the way back." The ringmaster offered her a gloved hand, the one free of his whip. He added a deep bow and Miranda's squint caught the glow of something hiding underneath his shirt.

"Thank you." She smiled and slipped her fingers into the satin. The glove curled around her hands, and the man led her away from the bear.

"Now," the ringmaster's voice lost its gravel. His words flowed like honey, and his fingers turned hot against hers. "You're here with your family today?"

"No." Miranda smiled and squinted. She leaned her head to one side, trying to see what glowed beneath his shirt. "I only meant I was separated from the crowd."

"Alone?" He snorted and gave her a look that put heat in her cheeks. "Such a pretty girl without anyone at all to escort her. That hardly seems right."

Miranda tensed as a shiver traced along her spine. The blush turned to a chill as the man's fingers shifted against hers, squeezing softly, sliding the fabric of his gloves across her skin. When she didn't answer, he laughed, tossing his head and making the glowing thing dance beneath his spangles. What was it? She squinted at him, and saw only shadows wrapped around that spark of light.

"Young girls should be careful," he said. "The circus is more serious than it appears."

She wanted to tell him that she knew that, to brag perhaps, about what her squinting had revealed. But she also heard a threat in his tone. Or perhaps, it was only a friendly warning. Miranda smiled for him, smiled like a girl who couldn't see a thing.

"Thank you," she said. "For getting me back on track."

"But of course."

The ringmaster led her, his ring of keys jangling at his hip, to the big top. He ushered her inside the ragged canvas while Miranda imagined what he hid beneath his spangles. She thanked him again and watched him slip away into the crowd, shaking hands as he went, bowing to either side.

But never low enough to show his secret.

Miranda's aunt had secrets too. They'd lived together since Miranda's thirteenth birthday, since her parents' death, and it hadn't taken a clever girl long to discover the things the old woman hid. Miranda had many questions, but like most adults, her aunt offered half answers, dodges and partial truths.

The old woman refused to enlighten her, and by sixteen, Miranda's patience expired. She'd taken the book, though many of the pages gave her a headache. She'd read what she could and filled in the rest with her own dreams.

Many truths can only be seen sideways, through half-open eyes. For it is the nature of magic to be hidden.

The circus bleachers had cracks, splinters that snagged at her skirt when she climbed them. Miranda chose a spot halfway up. She watched and squinted and imagined what sort of curse might turn a man into a bear.

Lights danced high in the tent. The crowds hushed, and Miranda's thoughts swirled inside a head hungry for magic. The elephants had none. The bareback rider's act held only luck and skill. Miranda watched each performance through eyes half open, judging, squinting, and, as often as she could, snatching a glimpse of the ringmaster's shirt.

The acts only played at sorcery, casting a different kind of spell over the crowd. One tightrope walker faltered to the rumble of snare drums, and according to Miranda's halfway vision, the trapeze artist flew without arcane assistance.

The circus lights dimmed. The colors faded.

At last, the ringmaster drifted to the center of the ring. He raised his arms, brought silence down along with them. Miranda scooted to the edge of her board, felt the bite of splinters, and narrowed her eyes. Glowing underneath the fabric of his shirt, something small.

"Ladies and Gentlemen!"

It moved when he gestured, swinging from side to side beneath the silk.

"Please welcome the star of our little show."

Miranda had come to the circus to find magic, lured by the music, the colors and the smells. She'd dreamed of acts that defied the laws of nature, of a show that would fit into her fancies. Sparkling costumes and dancing animals. Feats of strength and things of beauty. All the things that had proven to be illusions.

Except for the bear and his ringmaster.

Watching from her rickety perch, Miranda imagined dark crystals. She'd read about curses cast beneath the moon, rituals that might trap a human's soul in an animal's body. In her imagination, she paired those spells with childhood stories. Had the ringmaster used his glowing secret to imprison Boris? She imagined the story, painting the circus around her with fairytale strokes. The bear became a lost prince, and the ringmaster a jealous sorcerer.

"Boris the bear!"

He rode out through a red curtain, trailing it like a cape for just a moment. His feet pedaled the impossibly small unicycle, and Miranda hardly saw the bear at all. Her narrow vision revealed his true shape, and her imagination filled the gaps, weaving her prince into a story of betrayal and powerful magic.

The crowd gasped. The bear raced round the ring. The iron keys jangled at the ringmaster's hip, and the secret beneath his clothing glowed brighter. Miranda squinted and watched, certain on the third pass that Boris winked at her, that his eyes practically begged for help.

More than a bear entertained the crowd, and no one else could see it properly. No one else could break the prince's curse. No one besides Miranda, squinting and planning on the edge of her seat.

Miranda went to the circus for three straight days to learn the ringmaster's schedule. He haunted the wagons before the show, but after the final drum roll the man vanished from the grounds for at least an hour. The performers drifted here and there, but she could dodge them, make an excuse for lingering if caught.

Miranda sat in the back on the fourth day. She squinted at the spangled shirt and at the bear who was more than a bear, and she waited for the show to end. When the crowd filed out, Miranda shuffled with them, but she ducked from the mob before reaching the gates and retraced her steps between the carts. This time, she kept her eyes open and straight ahead. She kept a look out for the villain who had trapped a prince, and she moved her feet firmly, as if she belonged behind the scenes.

No one questioned her. The ordinary jugglers practiced by their cart. The fat lady smoked a cigar on a pile of tarps. Miranda might as well have been made of mist. Except that when she found the prince's cage again, he was already waiting for her.

Boris sat near the bars with his paws wrapped around the iron. He lowered his muzzle when Miranda crept near, and his soft eyes never left her. The prince only she could see had been waiting for her to come.

"I have to hurry." She whispered, suppressing a stutter of embarrassment and a brief surging of doubt that insisted he was only a bear. That vanished when the black lips moved.

"He'll be back soon." The bear's voice didn't growl as much as she'd expected.

"I want to help you." Miranda shifted her feet, didn't quite draw closer to the bars. "You *are* more than a bear, aren't you?"

"Yes." His huge head nodded. The little hat slid toward one ear. "I am much more than a bear."

Miranda's heart pounded. She looked into soft brown eyes and felt the magic tugging at her. "Were you cursed?"

"After a fashion." Boris shifted his grip on the bars and his claws clicked against the metal. "I trusted the wrong man, and fell under the spell of the circus and its master."

"And now you're trapped?" Miranda stared at his paws.

"I am."

"One of your claws is missing."

"You're a very clever girl."

Miranda straightened her spine, lifted her chin and looked her prince in the eye. "Can I help you break your curse?"

"The circus is threaded through with iron," Boris said. "But outside its boundary, I would be free of the ringmaster's chains."

Iron is the only thing that magic fears. Properly used, it can bind and break. It can hold and imprison.

A shiver writhed up Miranda's spine. If she could free him, would the magic turn him back into a prince? Her dream shifted again, painting herself as the hero. She stifled the urge to giggle, or to dance in place. But when the bear pressed his face closer to the bars, Miranda shivered.

He was larger than she'd remembered. His claws made dagger hooks around the bars, but his brown eyes felt like a warm blanket. Miranda nodded and answered with her eyes half open. "What can I do to help?"

In the books she'd read, the prince was always very grateful. If she freed him, perhaps Boris would reward her, teach her about the things no one else would say. Perhaps, he would free her, too.

"Come at midnight," the bear said. "They'll have passed out by then."

The between times.

Midnight. Miranda nodded. "Won't the gate be locked?"

"Behind the big top there's nothing but an old wire."

"Oh. Okay. Is there anything I should bring?"

"Does a girl who squints at the world own a gun?"

"No. Um. I don't, and my name is Miranda."

"Then bring only your courage, Miranda. And come back when the ringmaster's snoring rattles the wagons."

She stepped away, then paused and thought about the dark, the size of the bear, and the fact that bears shouldn't be *able* to speak to young women. No matter what her fairytales said. Miranda turned back for a final peek, but the bear with a prince inside lunged against the bars, pressed his huge muzzle through and growled with curling lips.

"Hurry. Go, girl!"

Miranda stumbled away, forgetting to care if anyone saw her. She jogged past the fat lady and the jugglers and saw only the blur of overly painted smiles as she went. She ran out of the gate, and not until the tent was a billowing mountain behind her did it occur to her that he hadn't sounded like a prince at all.

The circus looked different in the dark. The colors grayed, and the breeze made a snapping shadow of the big top tent. Miranda crept around the back, through the brambles which lined the parking lot and over a scattered collection of rocks and rubble cleared from the field.

She found the wire and slipped beneath it, aware of every crunching stone under her feet. Every whisk of her jacket arms sounded like a car alarm in the darkness, and every exhalation made her freeze and listen for the sounds of an angry ringmaster.

During the final hours of waiting, Miranda had thought of something she hadn't considered before. She'd wondered what a man who could make a prince into a bear might do to a girl caught sneaking through his circus after hours. As she slunk between the poles and looked, from one wagon to the next, Miranda's heart raced. Her resolve wavered, and she squinted over and over, looking for the glow that would mean the villain had found her.

At the back of Boris's wagon, Miranda stopped and caught her breath. He wanted her to let him out. Here in the darkness, Miranda understood exactly what he'd meant about courage. She reminded herself there was a prince inside him. There had to be a prince.

Her squinting had seen it.

Just when she'd convinced herself, when her lungs had settled and she'd decided to step into view, Boris spoke, right near her ear. "Are you ready?"

"Y-yes." So close, that voice, and not courtly in the least.

"I didn't think you'd come."

"I promised I would." Miranda peered into the cage, forgot to squint and lost her breath at the size of him. A wall of fur, a clattering of claws, but also the soft brown eyes that watched her from deep inside him. "Are you sure they're asleep?"

"Three bottles past drunk out of their minds," the bear said. "Passed out but for the fat lady who is... otherwise occupied."

"What do we do next?" Miranda thought, perhaps, she should have asked him about that earlier. She knew she should have when he spoke the next words.

"*You* get me the ringmaster's keys."

"Where are they?" She swallowed sawdust and pictured the glow beneath a spangled shirt, the long whip in a gloved fist. "I don't know..."

"His wagon is the closest to the gate. His door will be open, and the keys will be inside."

"Isn't *he* inside?" She couldn't do it. Miranda heard that much in the pitch of her words. She felt it, in the thumping of the heart inside her breast. "I can't."

Despite the stories, the magic, and her chance to be a hero, Miranda considered running back home as fast as she could and never, ever returning to the circus again.

"Miranda." The bear's eyes lowered, staring at her from behind his bars. His wide nose pressed against the metal, twitching, smelling her. "You forgot to squint."

"Oh." She closed her eyes halfway and found the prince's face still wore the same eyes. "Oh."

"You can do it, Miranda," he said. "You can free me."

The ringmaster's wagon had a metal step beneath the door. It had no bars, only painted walls and a narrow window on one end. Miranda hovered outside, listening to the sound of drunken snores.

Boris had been right about that.

Miranda inhaled slowly and reached for the door handle. She stepped up and

79

pressed her ear close to the wood. Snoring, loud and ragged from inside. She pulled the door open just enough, slipping into the wagon and a chaos of fabric and boxes. If there were shelves inside the ringmaster's cart, they'd long since spilled their contents. The detritus of circus theatre lined the miniature room and only a narrow aisle had been kept free.

That led to a low mattress, and upon that the ringmaster dreamt away his booze.

The first thing Miranda noticed was his bare chest. The second was the ring of iron, the keys dangling from a peg in the wall, easily within reach of the door. She could snatch them and be out in a breath. When she squinted at the scene, however, Miranda's attention was captured by the glowing amulet.

A single, sickle claw on a string around the ringmaster's neck.

Miranda had never been intoxicated, never had more to drink than a sip from a friend's glass. Just enough to let her know she didn't care for it. She had no idea how drunk a man had to be not to notice someone taking off his necklace.

The bear hadn't even mentioned it. She only needed the keys. But once that iron ring was in her grasp, Miranda's feet kept moving. Before she could think, she was leaning above the sleeping ringmaster, squinting at the claw and imagining a way to get it free.

Cutting the thong would be easiest, but a brief glance around suggested nothing which might sever the cord. She held her breath, reached her fingers for the amulet and lifted it from his smooth skin. Easy enough, except now she held the thing and the ringmaster's head still pinned it to his mattress.

Her hand wrapped around the claw. The glow transferred to her skin, made her fingers alien things. Miranda eased it over his head, watching his eyes, willing them to stay closed.

If only he'd roll over.

Warmth spread to her wrist, flaring, lifting all the little hairs along her arm. In his sleep, the ringmaster sighed and obeyed, rocking onto his side and freeing Miranda's prize from his possession.

Magic?

The bear claw hung in her grasp. The iron ring weighed heavily in her other hand. She didn't have time to wonder how these things had happened. Miranda backed to the ringmaster's door, froze in the entrance when he snorted and mumbled something she couldn't catch.

Don't wake up.

The claw warmed again. This time, she slid the thong over her head, put the amulet on and let the claw rest beneath her shirt. The ringmaster sighed, snorted, and Miranda eased out of his wagon and shut the door.

The step creaked when she descended. Something thumped inside the wagon. She clutched the keys to her chest and ran into the darkness. She quieted their jangling with her arm, silenced her heartbeat with a deep breath and raced to free the bear.

Boris waited, fur pressing through the bars and soft eyes shining. Miranda stopped beside the lock and raised the ring for her prince to examine.

"You did it." His voice held no surprise. "Quickly. It's the centermost key."

Her fingers fumbled with the heavy metal. Miranda pried the middle key from the group. She fit it, neatly into the lock. The darkness behind her spoke before she could turn it.

"I wouldn't do that."

The ringmaster had found them out. The bear's voice whispered near her ear, hissed through gleaming teeth.

"Open it."

"Boris is more than he appears," the ringmaster said.

"I know about that." Miranda tried to sound brave, but her eyes fixed on the bear's fangs.

"Do you?" A half dozen steps more and he'd stop her. Only a few breaths to decide.

"He's magic." She whispered it, but the sound carried in the dark, sounding too loud, harsh and too real. Adults didn't admit to magic, not outright, and now she'd look like a foolish child.

"He is." The ringmaster surprised her. "And magic can be very alluring."

"No one will talk about it." Her frustration put a tremble in the words. She turned her head, looking away from the bear.

"I will." The spangled shirt sparkled in the moonlight. Its owner took a step closer, spoke to her like no adult ever had. "Boris and I have a bargain, one made by blood and magic. He traded his freedom for my protection, and now he'd use you to break our promise."

"Liar." Boris growled. "You are made of trickery and lies."

"And you are a creature of magic, dangerous and desperate." The ringmaster scooted a step closer. "He is a monster, girl. A halfway thing. His prison is for our safety. Do you believe that he won't turn against you? That a thing of magic can ever be trusted?"

Miranda's hand shook. The keys rattled and shone in the moonlight. The ringmaster's voice flowed like the words in her aunt's book. They made her head hurt. She turned back to the cage. The iron bars gleamed beneath furry paws. She saw the wound, the stump where a claw should have sprouted.

"I..." Miranda's eyes lifted, caught her own reflection in the gaze of the bear prince. "I don't know."

"Please Miranda," he growled. "Save me."

Her hand moved. The key clicked in the lock. Around Miranda's neck, a single bear claw flared to life. It burned her skin. The iron bars swung open, and the girl dropped to her knees in the dirt.

The ringmaster's face grew moon pale. His mouth opened. Miranda saw him in slow motion, stretching to find his voice, to let his fear free. Boris was faster. Before the man could scream, the bear was on him. Before *Miranda* could scream, the ringmaster was dead.

She heard it in the crunching, the snap of bones, and she felt it in the heat of the amulet around her neck.

"Miranda?" Heavy feet padded against the earth. The darkness shifted, streaked with cinnamon. "Come out, Miranda."

In the space beneath the bear's wagon, Miranda cowered and shook her head even though he couldn't possibly see it. At least, she prayed he couldn't see it. Her hands gripped the claw in a vise, and her belly pressed to the cold dampness below the cage.

The long shadows. The halfway places.

"Miranda, we don't have time for this."

Miranda cringed when the muzzle appeared. The black nose twitched, caught her hiding, and Boris shifted his head to one side, pointing an eye at her that didn't seem so soft now.

"There you are." His lips curled when he spoke, showing large teeth. His voice growled with frustration. "What did you think would happen? He didn't mean to let us walk away."

"You killed him." Tears squeezed from the corners of her eyes. In the stories the prince never killed anyone.

"Yes." Boris blinked. "Thanks to you."

"W-what do you mean?"

"I never could have touched him if he'd worn that." The heat emanating from her new necklace confirmed his point. "Protection from bears. I sacrificed that claw in exchange for sanctuary, but my trust was misplaced. I was given a cage instead, a lifetime as a sideshow freak. So long as the ringmaster wore my claw, I couldn't harm him. Now you wear it, and there's no reason to remain in the filth."

"You're not a prince." Perhaps the knowledge of what she wore made her braver. Perhaps it was the certainty that she was not, not ever leaving the filth while the bear was out there.

"I never said I was."

"You di—"

"More than a bear," Boris said. "You'll remember. And I think we can agree it's true, unless you've spent other nights conversing with bears in the darkness."

"No." Had he given her half truths too? Or had she only half listened?

"I thought not." He blinked and grunted. His big body flattened to the earth, and his muzzle poked its way beneath the cart so that both his eyes could stare at her. "Are you coming out?"

"No."

"Now you believe I'm a monster?" His nose twitched above blood-stained lips. "But you know nothing of the torture I endured. Nothing of the man who died, either, a *cruel* man, free with his whip. I gave him an easy death, Miranda. It's a great deal more mercy than he showed me. A long life in a cage, imprisoned, trapped in this half of myself."

They stared at one another, the bear and the girl. Miranda tried to hear him, but her ears remembered the crunching, and her eyes pressed tightly closed.

"I see." His voice drifted as he pulled away. "Your fantasy has fractured."

"I don't know what you mean."

Keep your eyes shut. Don't listen to the claws against the stones.

"I mean that girls who squint at the world often see only what they want to."

Was that what had happened? Miranda felt the heat of Boris's claw against her breast. She lay on it, letting the warmth of the amulet ease her panic. Had she only imagined a prince? Had she freed a beast or a man? Seen his truth or her fiction? Embarrassment flooded through her, even stronger than her fear. Had she really only wanted half the truth?

"Last chance?" His words softened now, his footpads already leading him away. "Be brave, Miranda."

Her eyes fluttered open. Her dreams still whispered to her, but then, they'd only been half thought out. She watched Boris walk away, and if he shifted when he passed the circus boundary, if his furry outline smoothed and changed, she could almost convince herself she imagined it. The night fell silent as the bear vanished. After he'd gone, Miranda was alone in the darkness with a dead man, a ring of keys, and an empty cage.

In the morning, they found her locked inside the bear's wagon. A juggler discovered the key ring a few yards away. He set Miranda free while the police cleaned away the ringmaster's remains. When Miranda told her how the man had died, they all believed her. When she explained how the ringmaster had invited her back to his wagon, no one questioned. That he'd been drunk was never in doubt.

He'd boasted of his skill with Boris to impress her, had lured her to the bear's wagon for a private demonstration. When the beast went mad, Miranda said, she'd survived by locking herself inside his cage.

They believed her because she told the story with her eyes wide open.

They believed her even though they never found the bear.

And though Miranda never took off the amulet, eventually, she could almost believe her story too. She could almost forget the sound of bones crunching, the voice of a man who was more than a bear.

And she only ever squinted once, years later, when a man with soft brown eyes offered to buy her a drink. Then Miranda clutched her amulet and looked with eyes half open, to see if there might be a bear inside.

See Frances Pauli's story "With Eyes Half Open" online at Metaphorosis.
If you liked it, leave a comment. Authors love that!

Remember to subscribe to our e-mail updates so you'll know when new stories are posted.

About the story

"With Eyes Half Open" is the result of a writing prompt featuring circus-themed stories. I began with a young girl searching for magic, but as soon as Miranda walked through that gate, she was skeptical. The illusion of the lights and colors, the showiness and the theatrics did not impress her. I had to find something deeper, darker to capture her attention, and Boris the 'not quite a bear' stepped right in to lend a paw.

A question for the author

Q: If someone wanted to make an animated series out of your work, based on the title or recurring themes, what would it look like?

A: An animated series based on my work would look a great deal like studio Ghibli meets Disney's Zootopia . I populate my worlds with talking animals, fairy tale themes, and a touch of humor. Miranda from "With Eyes Half Open", would certainly love to be a Ghibli girl.

About the author

Frances Pauli originally studied visual arts. She still wanders from time to time between the canvas and the blank page, but for the most part has settled herself down to tell stories. A lifetime resident of Washington State, she currently resides in the central desert with her family and a host of unusual pets. Her work is almost always in one of the speculative fiction genres and more often than not features animal characters.

francespauli.com, @mothindarkness

A Sacrifice for the Queen

Luke Murphy

Long before dawn I give up trying to sleep and walk around the apartment packing some essentials into a travel bag. If things go badly today, I'm prepared. As I'm putting my government passport into my purse, a wave of nausea sloshes through my guts. I make it to the toilet this time.

When the heaves subside, my phone buzzes with the first of the day's texts from the boss.

From Insindiso, Queen of Toronto, to her loyal servant Karen Chen, greetings. I do regret that you are ill. Are you fit to work today?

I put my mouth under the tap and rinse. "Just the usual morning sickness, your Majesty," I say. "That's probably it for the day."

If I can be of assistance, please let me know.

"Thank you, ma'am, I appreciate your concern." Especially since she was opposed to my pregnancy. Six weeks ago, I told her what I was planning. *I strongly urge you to wait until the current crisis has passed, she said.* I might have. But then my Mum called to remind me that I'm thirty-seven and single and still haven't given her any grandchildren. I brought my gay best friend Marcus over that evening and held his free hand while he masturbated into a turkey baster and we giggled at the porno video. Now tiny, perfect Peanut is growing inside me.

And I still have the most stressful job in the city: the public face of Queen Insindiso.

Don't worry, Peanut. If I still have a city tomorrow, I'll hand in my notice. Let's just get through today.

My phone buzzes again as I pour a mug of coffee. (Decaf now. Such sacrifices I make for you, Peanut.)

Karen, she texts, *I request your counsel concerning Kokheli, the Usurper of Detroit.*

I open my laptop and check the news feeds. Footage shows the sun rising on the bodies of a dozen men and women hanging from the Ambassador Bridge. In confession videos, they weep and babble about their plot to overthrow Kokheli, and beg her for mercy. They got it. Hanging's better than the alternative.

The Usurper's been tightening her rule since her decree that all able-bodied subjects aged between sixteen and fifty are to work on building her temple. Every night a few people escape into the United States or cross the river into Canada, but far more get caught by Kokheli or her daughter.

"Breaking news," says the anchor. "Kokheli is now demanding two extra human sacrifices every full moon until her temple is complete. Let's get a comment on this—"

I pause it.

"Has Kokheli responded yet to your ultimatum?" I ask.

She has just now rejected it, texts the Queen. *By the ancient customs of my grandmothers, I see no alternative to a duel.*

"The people won't support this, ma'am."

Do they not love and trust their Queen?

"Not when your customs risk their future."

I made an oath to my grandmothers that I would respect their ways. I cannot break that promise as long as I live.

"Love and trust must be repaid, ma'am. You need to show that you listen."

Before me, people were murdered. Assaulted. Abused in their homes and workplaces.

"I was one of them."

I brought justice and equality.

"True."

And I let them protest outside my very palace.

Only because I persuaded her to allow it. "Ma'am, fight this duel if you must. If you prevail..."

I know what you want, dear Karen. A citizen's assembly, political parties, a constitution.

"And we still can't have them?"

The Queen's rule is absolute and for life. So say the customs. I cannot change that.

I throw up my hands. One way or the other, I'm out of this job tomorrow.

"If you say so, ma'am. Do you still believe you'll beat Kokheli?"

Insindiso texts me a picture: cheering crowds surrounding her palace, fireworks blooming in the night sky. The image is blurry and the colours over-bright, like all of her visions.

I forward it to the press office and tell them to circulate it to the media. By tomorrow, Detroit will be saved, Insindiso will still be Queen of Toronto, and I'll ask to be transferred to a cushy job in the Foreign Ministry. Or, if her prophecy is wrong: Insindiso will be dead, the tyrant Kokheli will be marching into Toronto, and, if I plan things properly, Peanut and I will be safe and far away.

"I'll draft the challenge."

To ensure victory, I shall require the life of one of my loyal subjects.

"No." I slam my cup down and slop coffee onto the table. "We don't do human sacrifice."

If you wish your Queen to triumph in this duel, a sacrifice is demanded.

"Then what's the difference between you and Kokheli?"

Go to Detroit and serve her, if you wish.

"Please, ma'am. Don't do it. This is wrong."

The decision is made, Karen. Good day.

Why? Why is Insindiso now reviving the blood rituals of her ancestors?

Because she's afraid. She doesn't think she can win.

My phone rings. It's my mother.

"Karen? The Queen going to win or not? Canada keeping the borders closed."

I check the status online. They're only allowing government employees and diplomats to cross Toronto's border with Canada.

"Mum, the Queen says she'll win. And she's never wrong."

"Sometimes wrong."

"If so, I've got a plan. I have to go." I hang up and text Mick in Security. He owes me.

Mick: sign out a good car. Check wheels, brakes, etc. Fuel up and bring spare gas. Stay close to me all day.

After two scrambled eggs on toast and a shower, I'm dodging through the swarms of business people bursting from the subway entrances. Heads are down, faces tight. I check the Toronto Star's website. *Queen foresees victory over Usurper* is the headline over the blurry vision of her triumph, but nobody will feel safe until Kokheli is dead.

The Palace glitters in the early light like a great silver nail pinning earth to sky. Queen Insindiso built it on the plaza in front of City Hall from stone blocks cut in complex shapes. Its windowless, doorless skin is covered in spirals of tiny mirrors and glass beads.

I walk into Palace Square under the ornamental arch of crushed missiles and artillery shells. When I was ten I watched the Queen pluck them out of the sky on the day she and her people arrived. At the base of the Palace, the dozen shaven-headed cultists of the Children of Insindiso chant the dawn worship. They're extra loud today, trying and failing to drown out the couple of hundred protesters who have already gathered under the plaque commemorating the Treaty with Canada.

"Two! Four! Six! Eight! Change your ways or abdicate!" they shout. A news camera from CityTV pans across the crowd; I recognize a couple of Canadian spies among them. A young women at the edge of the protest spots me and runs over. I speed up my pace.

"Hey! Chen!" she says. "You tell the Queen to quit this crap, eh?"

"She can hear you. But yes, I'll pass on your concerns." As if it'll do any good.

"She loses this fight, we're all slaves!" the woman shouts at my back as I push open the door of Toronto City Hall.

Inside, the other members of the Queen's Council got the word and are waiting in my office.

"So the fight's on?" says the Foreign Minister.

"It's medieval," says my deputy, Dario.

"If we ditch the old ways, we could join the Rotterdam Group," says the Trade Minister. "Shenzhen's in too now. Nairobi's applied."

"Forget it," I say. "She never breaks an oath."

"And she wants a sacrifice?" says Dario. "Seriously."

"Can't do it," says Trade. "If we start sacrificing, we'll be kicked out of half our alliances."

"So we'll try to keep it secret," I say. I text a name to her. *How about him?*

For eighteen years I've avoided thinking of that name, but now I'm flashing back to that midnight in a stairwell in a U of T dorm. The guy from Engineering who I'd said no to the week before was suddenly behind me. He shoved me into the corner.

My head smacked the wall. Blood in my mouth. His hand on my throat. He drew back a fist. He was wearing gloves, I realized in that moment, because he had planned this. I flinched.

The punch never came. He cannoned into the air and cracked against the ceiling. A tendril of white mist held him. He screamed and thrashed as the mist pulled him through an emergency exit. The door slammed. As I sank to the floor, my phone beeped. It was the first time the Queen ever contacted me, and it was the number for a sexual assault support line. The next day, the guy was in a cell doing the Path of Solitary Reflection, and I applied for an internship in the Queen's government.

She texts me back.

Our sacrifice must give themselves of their own free will. He will not.

Damn. "I'll figure something out," I tell the room. "Say nothing about it to anyone."

"What if she loses anyway?" Dario says.

"Emergency plan," Trade says. "We run for Albany."

"Have they confirmed?"

"If we make it there," Foreign says, "we can set up a government in exile."

Don't worry, Peanut. If the Queen dies, I'm done. We're not going to Albany.

"Media's waiting for you in the press room," Dario says. I check my reflection on my phone and straighten my hair.

Cameras clatter and flash as I step onto the podium.

"Good morning." I hope I don't look as tired as I feel. "Her Majesty Insindiso, Queen of Toronto, issues the following statement. To Kokheli, the Usurper of Detroit: You have illegally overthrown my cousin Uvuko and have refused all demands to relinquish your false claim. I challenge you to single combat according to the customs of our people. Projectiles, firearms, and such weapons are forbidden."

Through a rush of shouted questions, I hear my phone buzz. I read the latest message and wave for silence.

"Her Majesty adds that she wants a tribute of two dozen shipping containers to be brought to Palace Square immediately. Sorry, I'm not taking questions."

I'm on the phone as soon as I step off the podium, getting the square cleared, telling Traffic to prepare. Within fifteen minutes I've got two freight company owners ordering every available truck to load up.

"Karen?" Dario is at the door of my office. "Watch." He brings up a news channel on the big screen.

A reporter is standing outside the borders of Detroit. In the background the half-built temple towers above the ruins of the GM building.

"– has accepted the challenge. Kokheli said that she will meet Insindiso later today on a field midway between the queendoms of Toronto and Detroit on neutral Canadian territory. We have cameras on their way to that field at this time–"

My phone buzzes. *Please come down to the square and help me don my armour.*

"Dario, find out who owns the field and offer compensation. Get Foreign to coordinate with the RCMP. They need to shut down the highway and clear the fight zone. And change that tie. You'll be her spokesperson there."

"Aren't you going?" he says.

"We can't send the whole government to watch a fight. Someone's got to manage things here." Someone with a child in her belly.

When he's out of earshot I call Mick. "Is the car ready?"

"Standing by."

"Great. There's a travel bag in my office. Could you put it in the trunk?"

An email comes in from a lawyer in Montreal. He confirms that my paperwork's in place. Even if everything else is lost, Peanut, we're going to be safe.

Beloved Karen Chen, are you planning to flee?

"Only if you lose, ma'am."

Do you not have faith in my visions?

"Faith is for people who don't have a baby to worry about. Let's get you dressed."

Downstairs, a stack of steel shipping containers the size of a mansion has risen in the square. The guards have ushered all the people to behind a ring of security barriers, except for the dozen cultists sitting cross-legged at the foot of the Palace.

"We're not going," shouts one. "We stay with our Queen."

"Get behind that barrier," snaps a guard. "I will drag you if I have to."

I put a hand on his arm. "You don't have to." I have an idea. "Children of Insindiso, Her Majesty has a special demand today that I think one of you may be willing to fulfill."

Two dozen wide eyes are on me. I ask the guards to leave us and gather the cultists into a tight huddle.

Three minutes later, I've picked the sanest looking one for what he promises me is the greatest honour of his life. The others are sworn to secrecy, and they march to the barriers at the edge of the square singing 'Hail Glorious Insindiso'. They join the growing throngs from the surrounding offices and shops who have come to see the Queen prepare for battle.

A faint hum fills the air. Around the high tip of the glittering spike, a pale mist is growing, becoming denser. The Queen is gathering her body. From the edges of her territory, from the skyscrapers and strip malls, ravines and alleys, schoolrooms and barrooms and bedrooms of Toronto, trillions of nanoscopic creatures are flying back to the Palace. The swarm of drones is her eyes, ears, and hands, and she needs every part of herself here.

Misty strands converge from all sides on the top of the Palace. The white cloud there is dense now, most of her tiny drones gathered. Tendrils reach down from the cloud and swirl around the shipping containers. Metal scrapes and clangs. Two containers lift into the air and hover with a gentle sway six storeys above my head, held by the cloud of drones. With a creak and groan, both containers implode, flattening into plates. A bolt plummets. An arm of mist grabs it in midair and sets it gently on the ground.

Another container levitates off the stack, and three more follow it. Screams of tearing metal echo around the square. The Queen squashes them into ribs, rolls them into cylinders, knots them into hinged joints. Flakes of rust rain down. At the joins, the mist presses so hard that a sharp smell of hot steel fills the square as the edges melt into each other.

Dario brings me a sandwich as the Queen sets the sixth and final leg into place. A clang echoes, then silence. A great steel insect stands in Palace Square, its shadow blocking out the sky. Patches of graffiti and logos of rail companies mottle its ribs and belly.

A cheer grows among the bystanders and resolves into a chant.

"In-sin-di-so! In-sin-di-so!"

In one corner, almost as loudly, the protesters shout "De-moc-ra-cy!"

The cloud of mist gathers again at the peak of the Palace. The Queen built her residence like a chimney, only open at the top, and down inside it the swarm descends. The Queen emerges naked. Floating atop a pillar of mist, she presents herself to her people.

She is just a brain, no bigger than a human's. A dot at this distance. She and her kind discarded their insectile bodies long ago and created the drones to serve them. As always, when she's exposed, I tense at the thought of what a bullet could do to that pale ball of meat. But many of her drones are still spread wide, watching everything. In her city nobody could harm her.

"Whose lives? Our lives!" shout the protestors. "Whose city? Our city!" A bullhorn voice calls for strikes and marches.

With a clang, the swarm swings open a hatch in the back of the insect's head. The Queen passes inside and the door creaks shut behind her. All over the insect, white tendrils reach into iron limbs and joints. A creak, a scrape: her swarm brings the armour to life. Legs take a cautious step. An iron head the size of a bus turns and nods towards me.

"Dario?" I say, and swallow the last of my sandwich. "Send the cars up. Time for you to go."

Karen, she texts, *do you know that I trust you above all?*

Oh, God damn.

Today of all days I need you. When all seems dark, be close to me.

I've never disobeyed her. I won't start today. I mutter, "As you wish, ma'am." I turn to Dario. "Change of plan. You stay. I'm going."

Tonight, you will return to a free city. I assure you of this.

And if she's wrong? At this time tomorrow, Kokheli might celebrate her victory by picking fifty random citizens to burn on a pyre in front of City Hall.

And if she wins? The protests for democracy will grow. She won't concede, so her choices will be chaos or crackdown. There's no good future for this city, just different kinds of bad ones.

I text Mick: *Pick me up. We're going to see the fight.*

Clanks and booms echo off the skyscrapers as the great insect walks up Bay Street, towering over the crowds that gather on the sidewalks. Many cheer; some turn their backs. Our line of government cars follows close behind her. Traffic has been diverted from our path but we struggle to keep up with her strides. The car bumps over the craters that her feet are making in the asphalt. Great. Another strain on the maintenance budget.

Behind me, the sacrifice is sitting in the rear seat with a security guard. His name is Cliff, he says, and he used to be a derivatives trader for one of the big brokerages.

"See my nose here?" he says. "I've got no septum. Burned right through it with cocaine. Burned a lot of things. Then one morning my phone beeped. It was her. The Queen. She told me something and... I gave it all up. She told me where to go to get help, but the only healing I needed was to be close to her all the time. So I joined the others by the Palace and I never left. She's never spoken to me since but I know she loves my worship. I feel it." He clutches my shoulder. "I want you to scatter my ashes outside the Palace."

"I'll do that." If she wins. If not, you're better off dead.

My phone buzzes. *My cousin is joining us.*

We're driving along the emptied highway past the forested valley of the Humber River, where Uvuko has been living in exile since Kokheli hurled her out of Detroit. A great thud, and another: a giant figure is striding towards us through the trees. Uvuko has built a six-legged body like the Queen, but of tree trunks garlanded with leaves and ferns. She bows to her protector and follows us, shedding twigs on the road.

At the city border, the Canadian guards check passports rapidly and wave us through. My phone shows me a news update. In Detroit, Kokheli smashed an office building and made her armour from the ruins. Footage shows her emerging from clouds of dust, bristling with broken spikes of rebar. Leaving her daughter in charge, she waded the Detroit River and crawled into Canada on six immense legs of rubble. In a live helicopter shot, RCMP sirens clear a path ahead of her. A swinging leg rips the front off a house; a bunk bed falls into the garden. She never pauses.

A fist of fear grips my guts. Compassionate Insindiso faces a pitiless enemy. The Queen hasn't a chance.

Flashing lights and a line of news trucks tell me that we have reached the field. RCMP officers direct our cars to halt. Insindiso steps over pine trees at the edge of the highway and into the grassy pasture. Uvuko joins her. The Queen gestures to her cousin: stay here at the edge of the field. Uvuko can take no part in the duel.

The guard escorts Cliff out of the car. I pause to talk to Mick.

"Park on the shoulder over there." I point to the far side of the emptied highway. "Point it back towards Toronto. If the Queen dies, we'll run."

"We're regrouping in Albany?"

"We'll head that way." And then we'll turn off and make for the gates of Montreal, where I have allies. Where my asylum request is already filled out and I can apply for my mother to join me. Where little Peanut can grow inside me, far from the stress and futility of running a government in exile.

A distant boom shakes the ground, then another.

"What was that?" I say.

Mick points. "She's here."

Kokheli is a grey hulk hundreds of metres away at the far end of the field.

She squats and beats the ground rhythmically with her forefeet. Boom-boom, boom-boom: the earth is her war drum.

I walk off the highway into the field. The RCMP have set up a line of tape to corral us into a corner. A CNN reporter finds me.

"Do you feel confident about Insindiso's chances today?"

I haul on a smile and say, "The Queen foresees victory, and I trust her, as do—"

"Thanks, got to leave it there. It looks like the fight is going to begin."

Insindiso raises her head high and clanks towards her enemy. Love floods me like a monsoon. I've forgotten all the times she infuriated me with her traditions; I just want her to survive this. Cliff, the cultist, presses in next to me, tears trickling down his face.

"She's so beautiful," he whispers. "When will she need me? And how?"

My phone buzzes. *Instructions will come at the appropriate time.* She's in no hurry for a sacrifice. Maybe she's changed her mind.

Cliff smiles in rapture and mutters his prayers. I wish I had his stupid faith.

Queen Insindiso bows to Kokheli. The Usurper swaggers up and nods.

The two giants step back from each other and move in a cautious circle. Insindiso's iron body seems longer, but lighter. Kokheli's concrete mass is low and strong.

Kokheli lunges forward and swats at Insindiso with an arm of boulders. The Queen steps back, light and quick, and drives a kick into Kokheli's flank. Concrete shatters and thumps to the ground. I feel it through my feet. The Usurper rushes forward, head down like a bull. Again Insindiso dodges, but a moment too late. A mass of mortar bangs off one leg. She stumbles, one forefoot dented flat, and smashes a leg down onto her enemy's spine. Kokheli crashes to the ground and rolls to her feet, staggering back a few steps. A loose chunk of concrete flaps from a twisted reinforcement bar on her back. It snaps and falls from her. Beside me, Cliff cries out in joy.

Insindiso steps back two paces and lowers her body to the ground. Kokheli stamps in fury and tosses her head. The Queen waits in silence. Her enemy charges. The ground thunders.

Insindiso is still. My hands are on my mouth.

The hurtling mass is inches from Insindiso when she leaps. Metal shrieks. The Usurper passes under her as the Queen twists in the air and stamps on Kokheli's back. The earth booms and shakes, birds burst from a tree as it topples, and I grab a cameraman's arm to keep from falling.

Kokheli's head thrashes, but she is pinned to the ground. Insindiso seizes one of her midlegs and twists. In a cloud of concrete dust the Queen snaps the leg off and flings it aside. It rips a trench in the earth. Kokheli rolls her body, lashing out. Insindiso leaps off and steps lightly back. She raises herself to her full height, lifts her head. Surrender peacefully, she is saying.

Kokheli regards her in silence then bows her head. She approaches the Queen, staggering on her five legs, and kneels. As if she deserves mercy.

Insindiso looks down on her, brings her iron head close.

No, Queen. Don't let her live.

Insindiso's head turns a degree towards Uvuko, who stands silently near me. The Queen's cousin nods a fraction.

Leaves flutter from her tree trunk head. What is their secret?

Silence lies across the field. My phone buzzes. I don't take my eyes from Insindiso.

Kokheli raises her head. Jaws sag open, chunks of concrete sliding apart. Inside her mouth a pair of black rods slides forward. A cold wave of fear crashes over me.

Both heavy machine guns fire together. Flash, flash, flash: a fierce rattle rips the air. Bullets tear through Indindiso's head and burst out the back in a fountain of steel shards. The guns rake her again and again.

This is not happening, I think stupidly. Firearms are forbidden.

The spent guns make dry clicks. Their barrels glow red hot.

Insindiso's body is still standing. Maybe the swarm moved fast enough to protect her inside the head. The Queen is safe. She must be.

The steel insect makes a creaking sigh and collapses to its knees. Joints buckle and, like a tower toppling, the mass of metal falls on its side and crashes onto the clay.

The Queen is dead. Her leaderless swarm is lost.

Shouts and screams break the silence. Inside me, something is torn open. I feel it like a gushing wound in my heart and I clutch it as if I can stop my soul from bleeding. My mouth opens and tries to cry but can't.

Mick's hand is on my elbow. "Karen? Let's go."

When all seems dark, she said, *I want you close to me.*

I push his hand away. My Queen needs me now. She had a plan, Peanut. We have to trust her.

I kick off my heels, duck under the police tape, and run across the grass. Behind me someone shouts an order. I keep running. The ground trembles, twigs and bark rain down on me, and a great shadow passes overhead. Uvuko is charging at Kokheli.

A tree trunk foot stamps into the ground before me. I dodge around it. Behind me police voices are shouting, corralling the crowd, but I'm too far ahead. I weave around waist-deep ruts in the ruined earth and reach a dented steel foot. Thunder to my side: Uvuko charges the Usurper. Boulders and branches burst into the air. I press myself against the side of Insindiso's fallen leg as splinters rain down. The pale mist of her swarm still clings to the cold steel: her drones are immobile now, waiting for commands that will never come.

The enemies step back from each other and I run through ruts around Insindiso's back. My lungs heave. The ground jumps with another booming impact. Uvuko is hurled high into the air, trunks broken, branches raining down. The ground shakes as she lands, scrabbling on twisted legs to hurl herself forward again.

Before me is the back of Insindiso's head, shredded with fist-sized holes. I seize the hatch that she cut into the steel. It falls off its shattered hinge and slams onto my toes. Agony flashes. I don't care. I put my head inside.

The Queen is smeared in tatters on the steel. All that she was is now a few handfuls of broken flesh.

Why couldn't she see that the Usurper would cheat? A branch crashes to the grass behind me. Uvuko will die too, and by tomorrow Toronto will be a city of slaves. I clutch my belly. Get ready, Peanut. We'll run for the car as soon as the way is clear. Why didn't the Queen foresee this?

Maybe she did.

In the moment before she died, my phone buzzed. I take it out now.

Her last message.

To my beloved servant Karen: If there is one who will give up their life for their Queen, let them stand in my presence and say Ndiza.

Ndiza. It means I will.

I see her plan.

Oh God, no. My own life I would give up in a heartbeat. But Peanut too? Never. The tiny life inside me is bigger than the world.

But who else could it be?

Not me. Not Peanut.

But the Queen chose me. The one she trusts above all.

It has to happen now. Kokheli is vulnerable: I can surprise her. I have seconds.

I could run away now. Huddle in Montreal while the cities of Toronto and Detroit shudder under Kokheli's lash. Try not to think of the thousands sacrificed on the pyre or worked to death. And I could watch my little Peanut be born and come into the world and maybe my joy in that would be greater than the pain of knowing that I could have prevented it all.

Or I could accept this heavy crown and walk into a world of silent grief.

Tiny Peanut, I love you more than the world, but the world is too cruel for you to live in it.

"Ndiza."

The mist clinging to the metal whirls as if whipped by a furious wind. She told her swarm what to do.

Ribbons of mist rush towards me and tighten in a cyclone around my body. I'm sobbing. All I see is white, closing around me. Nanoscopic drones flood into my mouth, my nose, my ears. I'm so sorry, Peanut.

Then darkness and silence.

And light. My brain bursts into bloom: I see in all directions at once. My faithful drones are furiously building new paths inside my mind. Every instant new worlds of knowing are born in me. More drones linger in my armour, awaiting orders. I feel them in their trillions: my eyes, my ears, my hands, seeing and hearing and touching all.

My old flesh lies in the grass, the skull cut cleanly open and hollowed out. A tendril of my drones reaches out and gently touches the cooling belly. Inside me is a well brimming with black grief. When I have time and privacy I'll drink that water until the well's dry. But now I have to lock a cover on it.

Now I fight.

All eyes and cameras are on the two broken giants swatting at each other. Brave Uvuko gave me the distraction I needed.

Kokheli the Usurper drives a kick into my cousin's belly. Tree trunks snap like twigs. Uvuko's broken body soars and falls in an explosion of soil. It won't rise again. Kokheli limps towards her: she will destroy Uvuko's brain with a punch.

The Usurper pauses, seeing that all cameras are on her. She must have her moment of glory. She lurches to where I lie, stands over my fallen armour, and rears up in triumph.

My drones flow silently into my dented leg. The foot is crushed to a sharp point.

Kokheli claps her forefeet overhead, concrete booming off concrete. Behold, she is saying, I destroyed this Queen.

I strike. For the watching humans, eyes blink in the time it takes. The metal spear smashes under Kokheli's jaw. Concrete chunks shatter into pieces and plummet.

Her guns fall end over end. I drive further through the masonry. Her drones respond, pushing me back. My thrust barely slows. I have my full power behind it and her swarm is scattered. Steel rips through rock and into the black void of her head where her brain is held suspended in space. Here the swarm is densest. They throw themselves at the metal, tearing and pushing at it, but it is too late.

In those nanoseconds we speak to each other through our drones.

"Cunning bitch, Insindiso. I felt you die."

"I have loyal servants. Have you?"

"So you cheated too. You're no better than me."

"You could have seen this path. Arrogance blinds you."

The steel edge of my foot touches the flesh of her brain.

"Please," she says. "Spare my daughter."

"I will. Be at peace."

She accepts release. Her drones stop fighting me as my iron smashes through her brain. Her body falls to the earth.

Millions will celebrate this moment, but my armour shudders in sorrow as tons of rubble bury the remains of Karen Chen, destroying it and the secret it carried. I want to collapse and weep for you, poor Peanut.

But now life is duty. All duty. And I rise to my dented feet.

The field fills with shouts and cheers. I invite Kokheli's drones to join me. Gratefully, they flow into mine. I hear the journalists talking, see the footage on their screens: in Detroit, the people have burned Kokheli's temple. Her daughter hurled flaming cars at the crowd, but when she felt her mother die, she fled for the river. I made Kokheli a promise. I'll offer the daughter a life of solitary exile.

Faithful Uvuko bows her broken wooden head to me.

"I will keep your secret," her swarm whispers to mine. "You are Insindiso now."

"Let's let the people of our cities vote on whether they want us," I tell her.

"My cousin chose you wisely," she says, and strips trees to repair her armour.

The cultist is weeping with shame, his sacrifice rejected. I send him a message: *I do not want or need worship. Be free.*

The moon is high as I march home. There's work to do: a funeral to arrange, a constitution to draft, an election to plan. That starts tomorrow. Tonight the people gather on Palace Square to cheer and sing under a sky bursting with fireworks.

I send my swarm out into all corners of the city, to watch and protect, to advise and heal, to listen to the hopes and fears and dreams of all my children. This is why we died, Peanut, my love. I hope you can forgive me.

See Luke Murphy's story "A Sacrifice for the Queen" online at Metaphorosis.
If you liked it, leave a comment. Authors love that!
Remember to subscribe to our e-mail updates so you'll know when new stories are posted.

About the story

I wanted to submit a story to an anthology on the theme of alien invasions. I had a spark of an idea: I was intrigued by how, in the ancient world, a city might have its own deity. Athena, for example, was the goddess of Athens. I asked myself what that would look like in the modern world.

That spark didn't take fire, and I missed the deadline. But the idea continued to smoulder and I became more intrigued by the world decades after the invasion: what had changed and what was the same? How would humans relate to powerful alien rulers? And could a person ever know what it was like to have that power?

A question for the author

Q: Do you live near where you were born? Have you traveled much?

A: I was born in a city that no longer exists: West Berlin, during the Cold War. After the collapse of communist East Germany in 1989, Checkpoint Charlie and the Berlin Wall are just tourist attractions now. I like to revisit it as it once was by reading Len Deighton's spy novels of the era. I grew up in the city of Kilkenny in Ireland, where I went to Jonathan Swift's former school. Toronto's my home now, but I still love to travel and have lots of places I want to go. And some special places I'd love to go back to, like Istanbul, the Indian city of Udaipur, and a tiny village in the foothills of the French Pyrénées.

About the author

Luke Murphy was born in West Berlin, grew up in Ireland, and now lives in Toronto with his wife and daughter. He is a freelance animator and writer, with his TV work appearing on places like the Discovery Channel and Nickelodeon.

www.lukemurphy.com

Copyright

Metaphorosis Publishing

Metaphorosis offers beautifully written science fiction and fantasy. Our projects include:

Metaphorosis Magazine

Metaphorosis, a weekly magazine of SFF short stories, including stories from all the authors in this anthology. Find out more at magazine.metaphorosis.com, and sign up to be notified of new stories.

Metaphorosis Books

Recent books from Metaphorosis can be found at books.metaphorosis.com, and include:

Score

Best Vegan SFF of 2018

an SFF symphony

What if stories were written like music? *Score* is an anthology of stories written to an emotional score.

The best vegan science fiction and fantasy stories of 2018!

Metaphorosis 2018

Metaphorosis: Best of 2018

All the stories from *Metaphorosis* magazine's third year. Fifty-two great SFF stories.

The best science fiction and fantasy stories from *Metaphorosis* magazine's third year.

Metaphorosis 2017

Metaphorosis: Best of 2017

All the stories from *Metaphorosis* magazine's second year. Fifty-three great SFF stories.

The best science fiction and fantasy stories from *Metaphorosis* magazine's *second* year.

Metaphorosis 2016

Almost all the stories from *Metaphorosis* magazine's first year.

Metaphorosis: Best of 2016

The best science fiction and fantasy stories from *Metaphorosis* magazine's first year.

Reading 5X5

Reading 5X5

Five stories, five times

Twenty-five SFF authors, five base stories, five versions of each – see how different writers take on the same material, with stories in contemporary and high fantasy, soft and hard SF, and a mysterious 'other' category.

Writers' Edition

All the stories from the regular, readers' edition, plus two extra stories, the story seed, and authors' notes on writing. Over 100 pages of additional material specifically aimed at writers.

Best Vegan SFF of 2017

The best vegan science fiction and fantasy stories of 2017!

Best Vegan SFF of 2016

The best vegan science fiction and fantasy stories of 2016!

Susurrus

A darkly romantic story of magic, love, and suffering.